Room in Your Heart

A folktale from Bhutan

Original story by
Kunzang Choden

Illustrated by
Pema Tshering

To the east of Thimphu and west of Trongsa,
somewhere among the mountains high,
lived an old woman in a little house.

A gray cat,
a yellow dog and
a brown speckled hen
lived with her and shared her hearth.

One evening, as the sun
went down, the shadows grew tall
and dinner simmered on the stove,
a gentle voice suddenly called out,

“Night is falling.
Neypo shong gna?
(Is there room for me?)”

A ragged monk in robes of red
stood at her door.

The old woman welcomed him in
and gave him a place of honor
near her altar.

She stirred a pot on the stove
and was about to serve the food
when a hurried voice exclaimed,
"This letter must reach Trongsa without
delay, but my calves are on fire!
I am tired and must rest a while.
Neypo shong gna?"

An impatient young man
with bulging thighs stood at the door.
His name was Garba Lung gi Khorlo
(the courtier with wheels of wind).

The old woman welcomed him in.

She hung up her tea churn on a peg
on the wall, and made space for
Garba Lung gi Khorlo.

Then she went back to stirring
the dinner pot,
when a loud voice called,
"I have lost my yak.
Now it's too dark to see and I have
nowhere else to go.
Neypo shong gna?"

A woman with rosy cheeks,
wrapped in a yak-hair cloak
stood at the door.

The old woman welcomed her in.
She cleared a space under her shelf and
the visitor gratefully took her place.

Finally the old woman was
ready to serve dinner.

But there were more voices at the door.

"Our donkey refuses to move one more step.
We have pushed him far too
hard and now his poor old legs
are worn out.
We have to stop here tonight.
Neypo shong gna?"

Two men and a donkey
stood at the door.

The old woman looked at
all her guests and cheerfully said,
"Come on in and do your best."
So the men squeezed in.

They were just in time to share
the dinner in her pot.
She ladled out the contents:
one got a single bit of turnip leaf,
another a tiny piece of bone,
another got a drop of
soup and so on.

The guests savored their
dinner and licked their bowls clean.
Fed and rested, they thanked
the old woman.

"You have such a small house, and yet
you managed to fit us all in.
How did you do that?" they
wondered aloud.

The old woman smiled
a cheery smile.

But it was the gentle
monk who spoke.

"There will always be
room in your home,
as long as there is
room in your heart."

The End

A NOTE ON BHUTAN

The Kingdom of Bhutan sits on the eastern edge of the Himalayas. It borders China to the north and India to the south, east, and west. Here are some fun facts about Bhutan:

The Bhutanese people refer to their country as Drukyul, which translates to 'Land of the Thunder Dragon' in Bhutanese.

The goat-antelope or 'takin' is Bhutan's national animal. According to a popular legend, the takin was created by the folk hero Drukpa Kunley when he was asked by followers to perform a miracle at the end of a feast. Drukpa Kunley took a heap of cow and goat bones and reassembled them into a new animal—combining the head of a goat onto the body of a cow.

Traditionally, everyone in Bhutan celebrated their birthdays along with the king on New Year’s Day. These days, however, many people celebrate birthdays with their families and friends!

Bhutan uses a ‘Gross National Happiness’ (GNH) index to measure the nation’s prosperity. It is measured by its citizens’ happiness. Conservation of the environment is one of the four pillars enshrined in the philosophy of GNH.

Bhutan’s national airport is surrounded by the peaks of the Himalayas, and landing a plane there is so challenging that only very few pilots in the world are certified to do so!

There are no traffic lights anywhere in Bhutan! Bhutanese roads use traffic signs, are often one-way, and use roundabouts to manage the light traffic. Bhutan is the only country in the world that absorbs more carbon dioxide than it gives out.

Archery is the national sport of Bhutan, and it is very popular.

Until about sixty years ago, there were no hotels or guest houses in Bhutan. Travelers could ask to stay in anyone's house anywhere. *Room in Your Heart* was inspired by this tradition.

BEHIND THE SCENES

About the Author

Kunzang Choden was born in Tang in central Bhutan, where she spent her childhood. She presently lives in Tang Bumthang and is restoring her ancestral home, which is now a museum. She started her professional career as a teacher in rural Bhutan. Since the early 1990s, she has devoted her time to writing on a range of subjects related to Bhutan, its cultural beliefs, and its traditions.

About the Illustrator

Pema Tshering is a contemporary artist inspired by Bhutanese visual heritage. His work often explores Buddhist spirituality and its manifestations in everyday practices. He combines the richness of Bhutanese traditional art with modern artistic styles. He is a founding member of Voluntary Artist Studio (VAST) in Thimpu, which trains, inspires, and supports young Bhutanese artists.

KITAB WORLD